M de Angeli

DATE D

ÚP THE HILL

BY MARGUERITE DE ANGELI

DOUBLEDAY & COMPANY, INC., GARDEN CITY, NEW YORK

Books by
MARGUERITE DE ANGELI

BLACK FOX OF LORNE

BOOK OF NURSERY AND MOTHER GOOSE RHYMES

BRIGHT APRIL

COPPER-TOED BOOTS

DOOR IN THE WALL

ELIN'S AMERIKA

GOOSE GIRL

HENNER'S LYDIA

JARED'S ISLAND

JUST LIKE DAVID

BOOK OF FAVORITE HYMNS

THE OLD TESTAMENT

PETITE SUZANNE

A POCKET FULL OF POSIES

SKIPPACK SCHOOL

A SUMMER DAY WITH TED AND NINA

TED AND NINA GO TO THE GROCERY STORE

TED AND NINA SPEND A HAPPY RAINY DAY

TED AND NINA STORYBOOK

THEE, HANNAH!

UP THE HILL

YONIE WONDERNOSE

HOW TO PRONOUNCE THE FOREIGN WORDS
AND WHAT THEY MEAN

Aniela	Ahn-yell'a	girl's name
Babcia	Bob'cha	Grandmother
barszcz	barshch	beet soup
Bartoszek, Mrs.	Bar-to'shek	a neighbor
chrósty	hroo'sty	a crisp cake
Dziadek	Dja'dek	Grandfather
Kościuszko	Kos-chush'ko	the Polish patriot
Kraków	Kra'koof	a city in Poland
Krakowiak	Kra-kov'yak	a dance
Kubiak, Mr.	Coob'yak	head of the school
Kulpiński, Mr.	Cool-pin'skee	the baker's name
kutia	koot'ya	a sweet
Łowicz	Lo'veech	a province in Poland
Łukasiewicz	Look-a-sheeay'veech	inventor's name
Mamusia	Ma-moo'sha	Mother dear
pączki	ponch'kee	doughnuts
Pasterka	Pas-tair'ka	the Shepherd's Mass
pierniki	pee-air-neek'ee	a kind of small filled dumpling
pierożki	peer-air-osh'kee	another kind of dumpling
Pułaski	Poo-las'ky	Polish-American patriot
Sobieski	So-bi-es'kee	Polish king during latter 17th Century
Stanisław	Stan-ees'laf	Mama's brother
Staś	Stash	Tadek's friend
Świderski, Mr.	Shvee-dair'skee	the butcher's name

HOW TO PRONOUNCE THE FOREIGN WORDS
AND WHAT THEY MEAN

Święcicka	Shvyen-cheet'ska	Cecilia's last name
Tadek	Ta'dek	Aniela's brother
Takasz, Mr.	Ta'kash	a neighbor
Tatuś	Ta'toosh	Papa
Tatusienko	Ta-too-shen'ko	dearest Papa
Wesołych Swiąt	Ve-so'lih Svyont	Happy holidays
Wijek, Mr.	Vee'yek	a neighbor
Wujek	Voo'yek	Uncle
Wujenka	Voo-yen'ka	Aunt

HOW THE POLISH LETTERS SOUND IN ENGLISH

c	ts
cz,ć	ch as in church
sz,s	sh as in shade
dz	j as in jam
j	y as in year
w	v as in vat
rz,ż	g as the second g in garage
ó	oo as in boot
ch	ch as in Scotch word loch
ą,ę	nasal sounds as in French sont and en

To My Dear Friends

EDWARD *and* HEDWIG

Chapter One

TADEK stood by the bakery window, but instead of seeing what was inside, he was drawing in his mind the frost pattern that covered the lower part of it and that fringed out into fern and stars. Aniela knew what he was thinking; she nearly always knew what Tadek was thinking. Ever since that time when Aniela had been kept at home with a broken leg, she had known Tad wanted to draw everything he saw. He had drawn pictures for her to keep her happy and together they had laughed at his drawings of the clucking hens, of Papa playing the organ, and all the other funny things they could think of.

Aniela, too, thought the frost pattern was lovely, but she wanted more to see what was inside, so she stood on tiptoe and pressed her nose close to the glass to see through the clear part above the frost.

She could see glittering paper stars and colored hearts that hung from the ceiling. She could see the candy canes and the clear candy toys, the piles of cakes filled with prune jam, the poppy seed cakes, and, best of all, the gingerbread St. Nicholas, with pink sugar buttons and frosted beard.

"Oh!" sighed Aniela. "What lovely *pierniki!* And see, Tadzio, see the *chrósty!* Do you think Mamusia will have *chrósty?* Ummmm! It smells so good, and I am so hungry. Today, it seems as if night would never come."

Tadek sniffed as if he, too, might be hungry. They took one more look at the delicious cakes and one more sniff, then Tadek said, "Come, Aniela, it is a long walk up the hill. Soon the stars will be out, and then we can have our supper." The thought of supper made him break into a run, and Aniela had to run, too, or be left behind. To Aniela, it was wonderful to be down in the town with Tad. To be left behind — unthinkable! She ran.

Snow had fallen all one night and lay inches deep in the little Pennsylvania mining town. It crunched and squeaked as they ran, and a biting cold wind blew it about in the afternoon light. Everyone carried an armful of bundles and wreaths of green. Ropes of laurel were strung across the street from the lamp-posts. Bells jingled on the harness when a horse and sleigh passed. Rabbits and chickens, stiff with cold, geese and turkeys and sausages in links hung before the butcher shop, where they would tempt the passerby, for it was Christmas Eve. The butcher-shop window was covered with a whole forest of frost ferns, and only a rosy glow near the top told that Mr. Świderski was there behind the counter. Aniela caught up with Tad and they passed the shoemaker's window where already a small light was burning, because the sun was behind the hills.

It was cold! Around the corner and up the steep street they went toward home, the wind blowing hard, icy particles of snow in their faces. The pavement was so slippery, they had to take long, slow steps to keep from falling.

Around the corner, and up the hill again, and they were home.

"Look!" said Aniela, pointing up over the church steeple. "There it is! There is the first star!"

They stood for a moment gazing at the star as it twinkled in the clear winter sky, and each made a wish. Aniela wished for the cakes she had seen in Mr. Kulpiński's window. Tad wished he could learn to paint the sky and the star as it stood over the church steeple.

Then they ran into the house where Mama was waiting. "Come, Aniela, dear. Off with your things. Soon Father will be here, and Grandmother and Grandfather."

"Has Stan come home yet?" Aniela asked hopefully.

"Yes, Stan has come and is just over the way giving greeting to old Mrs. Bartoszek. Tad, more wood for the fire, if you please."

Stanisław was Mama's youngest brother, who was attending the University in Philadelphia and learning to be a doctor. Aniela wished he would hurry back. He always had exciting things to tell about his life in the city.

Aniela helped Mama put the food on the table: the fish in aspic jelly and the

plates of cakes cut in stars and crescents. There were *chrósty*, too, and the Christmas wafers that were to be shared. She knew as she set the dishes on the table that there was straw beneath the cloth so that all would remember the Babe who was born in a manger, and the reason for celebrating Christmas.

Mama put the *pieroźki*, (the tiny dumplings made of dried mushrooms folded into small squares of dough) into the *barszcz*, Aniela's favorite soup. And then she handed Aniela the *kutia* for dessert. *Kutia* is made of boiled wholewheat grains, with honey and scalded poppy seed that Mother had ground to a paste with a wooden masher in a large earthen bowl.

Tad brought in more wood, and as he was putting it into the fire, the front door opened and someone cried out:

"May He be praised!"

Mamusia called back, "Forever and ever!"

It was Grandfather and Grandmother. Then Father and Stanisław came in. The little parlor was filled with talking and laughing, with the cold breath of outdoors, and the glow from the coal stove. *Babcia*, Grandmother, came out to help carry in the plates of steaming soup and dumplings, and everyone sat down at the table.

Father rose, and taking a wafer, shared it with Babcia, saying as he did so, "May the Lord bless you, dear Babcia, and may you have the new cow you have been wanting so long."

"Thank you, my son. May He bless us all." Then she turned to *Dziadek*, Grandfather, saying, "May the Lord grant that we all meet here again next year!" and offered him a piece of wafer. Dziadek thanked her and in turn passed it to Mother. Mother tasted it, then turned to Stan.

"Dear brother," she said, "may you finish your course at the University with honor, and may you be the finest doctor in America."

When Aniela's turn came, she shared the wafer with Tadek and said to him, "I wish for you, dear Tadzio, that you may find a way to learn how to paint pictures as you would like to do."

"Painting is no way to make a living," Father said. Then he remembered that it was Christmas Eve and spoke more cheerfully. "There is to be a painter fellow here soon, to paint the empty wall in the church; maybe he will give you a job of work helping him!" He laughed, but Aniela thought to herself, "Perhaps he will! There might be a way. Perhaps Stan will help Tad when he is through, or perhaps even *I* can help!"

Just as they were about to eat. Wujek and Wujenka, Father's brother and his wife, came in.

"May He be praised!" they called.

"Forever and ever!" answered Father. "Do come and sit at the table. You are very welcome." Already Mama was moving the chairs and the dishes to make room for them.

"We shall upset your table," said Uncle. "You didn't expect us."

"You are most welcome just the same," said Mama. "You know our old saying: 'Whatever the house is supplied with, you're welcome to it,' and 'A guest in the house is God in the house.'"

More good wishes were shared and extra food brought in. They sat at the table a long time, laughing and talking. Finally Aniela begged to go out with Tad to sing carols and to carry the lighted star he had made.

"It is better for little girls to stay at home," said Father.

"But I shall not be so little a girl much longer. Please, Tatuś, please, Tatulu! Tatusienko! Please!" Aniela begged, and got up from the table to put her arms around her father's neck.

"Well," Father laughed, "since you are so eager to go, and you call me

11

your dear father, your dearest, *dearest* father, perhaps you can go for a little while. Come back when you hear the bull whistle blow at nine."

"If you are back on time, I will tell you a Christmas story before you go to bed," promised Wujek.

Aniela danced out of the room to get her coat and cap. Tad brought the star he had made of colored paper and lighted the candle in it. They bowed to Mama and kissed her hand to thank her for the supper.

Staś ran out of his house with his fiddle to join them, and when they started to sing in front of Mrs. Bartoszek's house, Sue Shemega came out, too. They sang first the old birds' carol that Aniela loved best. Father had written it down with the words and music as he remembered it from Poland.

There were many other carols they all knew well. They sang, with Staś fiddling, all the way down the street and away up the other side, but when Aniela heard the whistle she knew she must go home as she had promised. Sue went, too, and though the boys kept the star lantern, there was light from the moon, and from the lamplight shining from every cottage. Sounds of homemade music drifted out into the night, and stars twinkled in the frosty air. The moon was so bright, Aniela could see the whole town and the hills beyond. Though her feet were cold and her fingers numb, it was almost too beautiful to go in the house, but she had promised Daddy, and, besides, there would be the story.

"Now sit here on my lap, Aniela," Uncle said to her when she had taken off her coat and warmed her hands at the bright stove, "and I will tell you the story of the gray spider."

"Does Uncle mean that a story of a spider is a Christmas story?" Aniela asked.

"Wait and you shall see," said Uncle.

"The gray spider worked very hard every day making long strands of silk

that he wove into a web in which he caught troublesome flies. But he noticed that everyone turned away from him because, they said, he was so unpleasant to look at with his long, crooked legs and furry body. Of course the gray spider didn't believe that, because he had only the kindliest feelings for everybody. One day when he was crossing the stream he looked into the water, and there he saw himself as he really was.

" 'Oh,' he thought, 'I *am* very unpleasant to look at. I shall keep out of people's way.' He was very sad, and hid himself in the darkest corner of the stable. There he again began to work as he always had, weaving long strands of silk into webs and catching flies. The donkey and the ox and the sheep who lived in the stable thanked him for his kindness, because now they were no longer bothered with the buzzing flies. That made the spider very happy."

Aniela looked puzzled. "Is this a *Christmas* story, Uncle?" she asked again.

"Wait and see," Uncle answered, and went on.

"One night, exactly at midnight, the spider was wakened by a brilliant light. He looked about and saw that the light came from the manger where a tiny Child lay on the hay. The stable was filled with glory, and over the Child bent a beautiful mother. Behind her stood a man with a staff in his hand, and the ox and the donkey and all the white sheep were down on their knees.

"Suddenly a gust of cold wind swept through the stable and the Baby began to weep from the cold. The mother bent over Him but could not cover Him enough to keep Him warm. The little spider took his silken web and laid it at Mary's feet (for it was Mary), and Mary took up the web and covered the Baby with it. It was soft as thistledown and as warm as wool. The Child stopped his crying and smiled at the gray spider.

"Then Mary said, 'Little gray spider, for this great gift to the Babe you may have anything you wish.'

" 'Most of all,' said the spider, 'I wish to be beautiful.'

" 'That I cannot give you,' Mary answered. 'You must stay as you are for as long as you live. But this I can grant you. Whenever anyone sees a spider at evening, he will count it a good omen, and it shall bring him good fortune.'

"This made the spider very happy, and to this day, on Christmas Eve, we cover the Christmas tree with 'angel's hair' in memory of the little gray spider and his silken web."

Aniela clapped her hands. "Oh, that was a lovely Christmas story after all, Uncle. Now I shall never be afraid of spiders again."

"Now off to bed with you," said Mama. "When you wake at midnight and the bells are ringing, it will be your birthday, too, remember?"

Did she remember? Of course she remembered. Was she not named Aniela because she was born on Christmas just when the bells were ringing? Hadn't Mama said it seemed as if the angels were singing? Did not her name mean "angel"? She went off willingly enough, knowing that when she woke the Christmas tree would be standing in the corner of the little parlor, covered with hearts and bright balls and with *pierniki* and shimmering "angel's hair." Perhaps beneath it would be a gift for her and one for Tadek. She looked once more at the bright star and wished for Tadek that he could go to school where he would be taught to draw and to paint. The moonlight touched the little Madonna that had belonged to her great-grandmother. From the carved wooden frame that was like a little house, the Queen of Heaven with the Babe in her arms looked out on the world just as she had looked for a hundred years.

Chapter Two

BELLS! BELLS! Ringing! Ringing! BELLS! Caroling! Caroling! BELLS! Chiming! Chiming!

Aniela woke with a start and jumped out of bed and ran to the window. Christmas! It was Christmas! It was her birthday, too!

Aniela could almost see the angels fluttering around the bell tower, singing, as the happy music rang out! Perhaps they were real angels like the Angel Gabriel! Perhaps they were baby angels like the ones in the painting in the chapel. Aniela hurried down the stairs, where she heard Mother calling.

"Tadek! Aniela! It is time to go to church, to the Shepherd's Mass, the *Pasterka. Wesołych Świąt!* Happy holiday! Don't you know it is Christmas?" Aniela ran down the dark enclosed stairway, and Tad woke from the chair where he had fallen asleep. Father was already at the church, of course, because he had to play the organ.

Out of the corner of her eye Aniela could see the Christmas tree standing in the light from the window. She could even see the glint of the "angel's hair," but knew she must not look yet. After church was the time for that.

Tad yawned as he put on his jacket. He hadn't been asleep for long. He and Staś had kept up their caroling until almost midnight. Tad thought he would stay awake until the bells began to ring, but the warmth of the stove was too much for him, and he had fallen asleep, even with Mama there putting the last touches on the tree. Tad was a grown boy of fourteen, big enough to drive the mine mules, so it was all right for him to see that it was Mamusia's patient hands that trimmed the little tree. To see her put the packages under it, then stand for a moment looking to see if all was arranged as it should be.

"Come, Tad, wake up!" Mamusia tousled his head, then smoothed the hair in place. His eyes were only half open. He couldn't find the buttons of his jacket, and when Mamusia clapped his cap on his head, he walked in a daze after Aniela, who hurried down the snowy path and around the corner, looking up to the bell tower, hoping she might really see the angels. Tadek woke up in the frosty air, and he, too, stopped for a moment.

"Look! Aniela!" he said. "Look! It is like a Christmas card! See how all the church steeples stand against the sky! Look how blue it is!" He shut his eyes for a moment and made strange motions through the air with his mittened hand. Aniela knew that he was trying to put down in his memory what he saw.

The church was filled with the smell of pine boughs, with smoky incense, and with the odor of burning candles. Every nook and corner held their flickering light, and it gave movement to the figures painted on the wall spaces. At one side the wall was bare and waiting for the picture that Father said was to be painted there after Christmas.

Tadek whispered to Aniela as he sat down and pointed to the wall: "If only *I* could be the one to paint it!"

But he knew, and Aniela did, too, that the day after Christmas he would be back in the mine again and would be saying, "Gee! Haw! Get along there, Rosie!" to the mule who spent her life down deep in the mine. Tadek loved Rosie but he longed to be up in the light and have time to draw and paint.

By the time the service was over and the family was back in the little parlor, everyone was ready for the coffee Mama had made. Stan had brought an enormous box of candy from Philadelphia. Aniela had never seen such a box!

Then the packages must be opened. There were warm woolen socks for Tadek to wear inside his rubber boots, and a new shirt for Stan that Mamusia had made. For Aniela, a white flannel petticoat, with what she called "sewings" around the hem, and a new guimpe to wear with the jumper dress Mamusia had made over from the rose cashmere, whose sleeves had worn out.

All day long, on Christmas Day, Aniela and Tad went with other boys and girls of the neighborhood to sing carols. Stás and Sue went, too, and Cecilia and Michael. They went from house to house and sometimes were invited to come in. They were given cake to eat and sometimes a gift of money for the "Freedom Fund" that the teacher of the Saturday school had started. The boys and girls knew it was to help those in Poland who were trying to keep alive the spirit of liberty such as we have in America.

Christmas Day ended all too soon. It was the end of Aniela's birthday, too, but though it was gone, it left her one year older. Now she was ten!

"Old enough," said Mama, "to have the fire well started, the beds made, the rooms in order, and the supper well begun when I get home from the factory."

Aniela looked ashamed. She knew that sometimes she forgot to smooth Tad's cot at all. She knew that Mamusia worked hard to keep her looking nice for school. Four days a week she went to work in a shirt factory. Father got very little for playing the organ in church, and of late there seemed to be few weddings where he could earn a bit extra. He had several pupils whom he taught, and sometimes there was a dance in the big hall, when he played for hours while the young people had a good time. But it was not enough.

Tad earned five dollars a week driving the mule, but there was rent to pay, coal and food to buy for the family. Besides, there was Stan just finishing his course at the University. He helped to earn his way by doing many things at the college: waiting on table, translating articles for the Polish newspaper, and tutoring students in Latin.

During Christmas week there was the entertainment by the Saturday school. Aniela was one of the angels, and Tadek was King Herod. He had helped one or two evenings making scenery, too, and Aniela was very proud of him. Anything Tad did was just right for Aniela.

Father played the piano when they sang the carols. All the fathers and mothers were there, and a strange man who sat with Father Witkowski, the pastor. He sang with the others and seemed to enjoy the party a great deal, and Aniela wondered who he was.

Most of the children whose parents had come from Poland went to the Saturday school. There they were taught the history of Poland and how for a thousand years the people of Poland had loved liberty and the right to speak freely as they chose. They spoke in the Polish language and were taught the grammar and the old songs of Poland.

"Let us keep the language fresh in our minds," said Mr. Kubiak, who was head of the school. "It is a beautiful one. It is pleasant, too, for those who are older, to hear the language they know, so let us remember it."

Aniela liked to go to Saturday school. It was fun to sing the songs and Miss Sadowska was teaching her fancywork. She had tried to finish her embroidered table cover for Mama for Christmas, but it was slow work, and when she tried to do it at home, she made so many mistakes that she had to take it all out again. So it wasn't finished. But more than the songs, or the embroidery, Aniela loved the folk dances Miss Sadowska taught them.

Sometimes Tad went to the Saturday school, too. The teacher had noticed that he liked to draw and tried to help him.

"Of course I know nothing of drawing," the teacher said, "except this.

Draw what you see around you, instead of **trying to do things you have never** seen. Everything is interesting if you make it so. If you draw what you see and know, it will tell a story."

So Tadek saw pictures in everything: in the soot-covered houses that stood near the mines, in the wheels that turned at the top of the shaft, in Babcia feeding her geese. Father thought Tadek was wasting time on drawing, but he thought the Saturday school a fine thing. Much as he wanted Tadek and Aniela to speak good English, he wanted them to remember their native tongue, and to be thankful that they were free to speak it in America.

"You know," he said, "where I went to school in Poland, we were not allowed to speak our own language, so we kept it alive in secret. When the schoolmaster thought it safe, we were taught the old songs of Poland, the long history of splendid things that had been done by the Poles, and we spoke in our own language. A boy was put on guard to give warning if an inspector should appear, and when the warning came, what a scurry there was! Every Polish book was hidden in a secret place and the other books came out. When the inspector came into the room, we were very busy doing whatever we were supposed to do. The smartest child was called upon to recite, and the inspector went away pleased. When he was well away and out of hearing, how we did shout and sing! And all this is why we have Saturday school in this free country."

Though it was Christmas week, Mama went each day to the factory. Aniela hurried to get through the work she was expected to do. Sometimes she remembered that she was ten and did her work more carefully. Then she went coasting with Sue down the twisting street, or she went down into the town with Cecilia, where they picked out the things in the store windows they would like to have.

Tad had gone back to work the day after Christmas. As he plodded up the hill to the mine, he thought about Rosie, the mule, and wondered if she had been well treated while he had been away. She was headstrong and needed Tad's special care to make her willing to work. He knew just how to manage her. By coaxing and gentle talk, he could get her started. He whispered into her ear and rubbed her nose. He fed her bits of sugar and pieces of cake from his lunch pail, and she worked with no trouble at all.

Tad was very proud of the way he could manage Rosie. He chuckled when Edwin Llewelyn told him how she had balked and refused to work for him the day before Christmas. She had snapped at him, too, when he put the feed in her box.

Tad chuckled, but already he was thinking of something else. He was wondering how he could draw Edwin Llewelyn's head with the light of the mine lamp in his cap glowing in the dark. All day he thought of it.

When he reached home, Aniela was in the kitchen putting chips into the stove to start up the fire. She laughed as hard as Tad when he told her how Rosie had balked. Then he told her how Edwin Llewelyn's face glowed in the light from the mine lamp.

"If I could just get hold of some paints," he said, "I know I could make a fine picture of him, and I could paint Rosie, too, with her long ears. I can just see how to do it!" He screwed up one eye and drew the picture in the air.

Chapter Three

ONCE, DURING THE HOLIDAYS, Mama had a free day so she took Aniela to visit Grandmother and Grandfather.

It wasn't far to Babcia's, just a good walk over the hills to the next valley. Dziadek had bought an old stone house with deep windows, where Babcia kept plants growing. The house was set in a few acres where they kept chickens and a flock of snowy white geese, whose soft feathers Babcia used to make pillows and feather beds. Babcia longed for a cow, too.

Aniela loved to go to Babcia's. The mine shaft was out of sight, and there was a clear, smooth field where Aniela could slide downhill without fear of horses and wagons and without running into tin cans or old bottles. Grandfather kept the field clean and ready for spring planting.

When it was time to plant, he took the seeds to be blessed, so they would yield a good harvest. He said a prayer as he planted, too.

"For," he said, "without God one cannot even cross the threshold."

He always told Aniela stories of the old country. How he used to build a platform with an old wagon wheel near the chimney on the thatched roof, hoping a stork would come to build a nest there. How the stork would tramp around trying the platform to see that it was firm, then settle down to build the nest, leaving for the winter, and coming back each spring.

When suppertime came Babcia sent Aniela to a neighbor for milk.

"Just wait!" she said, as she put her work-worn hand on Aniela's bright head: "we shall have that cow yet! Then, my Anielcia, you shall have all the milk you want. Take these eggs to pay for the milk. You know, Anielcia, we have plenty of eggs these days. If you like, you could sell some, and for every dozen you sell, I will give you three cents. Would you like to do that?"

"Oh, yes, Babcia! I could sell lots of them. Oh, I think that would be fun!"

As Aniela turned to go out of the kitchen, she knocked a loaf of bread onto the floor with her elbow.

"Tch! Tch!" said Babcia, picking it up and kissing it. "We must be careful

with bread. God gives it every day. Therefore, it is holy." She brushed the loaf carefully and set it back on the table. The bread, Babcia's own, was made of whole rye flour and caraway seeds and baked in large, round loaves. It was very crusty and good.

When supper was over, Dziadek took Aniela on his knee and told her more about his old home in Poland. How bitter cold it was in winter! How the wolves howled in the forest! Sometimes they came right into the village when they were very hungry. Then he told Aniela how beautiful the country was in summer, when the fields were planted, and each house in the village had its flower garden.

"We used to gather great mushrooms in the fall and dry them for cooking."

"Like we have in spring down in the meadow?" asked Aniela.

"Oh, no," said Dziadek, "much larger than those, and with a flavor so good and so fine that when they were cooking the delicious odor slipped out of the pot and drifted all over the house. It made the mouth water. It brought us all out into the kitchen where the mother was cooking to see if we couldn't hurry things along a bit." Just then Babcia heard him and turned from her dishwashing.

"Yes, that is so!" she said. "Always, when I am cooking, there must be all men and boys of the house underfoot in my kitchen. Especially if it is the little dumplings I am cooking."

"I remember that kind of mushrooms," said Mama. "They grow only in the deep woods where there is leaf mold and plenty of shade. And I remember how in the spring the frogs used to croak, and we thought they said, 'What's the news, what's the news?' and the others would answer, 'The stork is dead, the stork is dead.' Then the whole chorus would sing 'Hurray! Hurray!' "

They all laughed, and Aniela said, "I thought they said, 'Jug-a-rum, jug-a-rum'!"

When Aniela went to bed on Grandmother's high-piled feather tick, she noticed in the candlelight that the embroidery on the cover was the same pattern as her fancywork. She said her prayers before the little picture of the Queen of Heaven, and though it was a different Madonna from the one at home she wore the same quiet smile, the same comforting look.

Perhaps, Aniela thought as she snuggled down under the comforter, I can save enough from the egg money to buy Tad some paints!

The next day Mama had to leave early for the mill, but Aniela stayed until it was time to go to the Saturday school. Babcia filled a basket with eggs for her to sell. She sold them at the school, to Mr. Kubiak and to Miss Sadowska. She knew she must be very careful not to lose the egg money, so she tied it in the corner of her handkerchief, and it made her feel quite rich. She would put Babcia's money under the bust of Kościuszko, because it was hollow. Her own she would keep in the pig bank on the shelf in her room.

She told Miss Sadowska about Babcia's feather bedcover and how the pattern was like the one she was embroidering.

New Year's Day came with more visiting among friends and relatives. Then the holidays were over, and it was time for school to begin. The crisp winter weather turned suddenly warm and filled the valley with fog and mist.

One morning, when Tad got up in the cold dark to put on his working clothes, it was raining. As he left home, Staś came from his house, Mr. Takasz came from his, and Mr. Wijek from the one next door.

Around the corner and down the hill a little way Jim McCarthy, Mr. McGinnis, and Mr. Dougherty were also starting out for work. Edwin Llewelyn and many others joined the procession of men and boys on their way to the mines. They walked like dark shadows in the downpour that washed over the coal-streaked snow and ran in a muddy river down the roadway.

Tad sloshed through it with mud-caked boots, his shoulders hunched to keep the rain out of his neck. He was used to it, and to many other discomforts, so he hardly noticed it. Instead, he was thinking, as always, of how he could draw what he saw. The purple hills through the mist, the men trudging to work, the mine shaft and the turning wheels. Suddenly there was a spurt of steam as the whistle sounded for seven o'clock. Tad stopped day-dreaming and hurried to work.

The deep sound of the seven o'clock whistle woke Aniela.

It told her that it was time for her to get up. She could hear Papa out in the yard chopping wood and Mama's hurried steps as she got ready to leave for the mill. Just then Mama called up the stair:

"Are you ready for your breakfast, Aniela?"

"Yes, Mamusia, yes, I am coming," Aniela answered, and rolled over to the edge of the bed. Mama still stood at the foot of the stairs. Aniela could hear

29

the small sounds as she pulled on her rubbers. Mama called again.

"Aniela, are you up?" Aniela jumped.

"Yes, Mamusia, I am up!" And she was up. She heard Mama close the front door as she went out and knew she must hurry.

School! School began today. There would be more tiresome English grammar again, more words to learn in spelling that looked so much alike and sounded so different. She would never forget how hard it was to learn that the "o-u-g-h" in "through," "rough," and "trough" all had different sounds; how hard it was to remember the difference between "bear"—an animal; "bear"—to carry, and "bare" meaning without covering.

In spite of that, Aniela was rather glad to go back to school. She was fond of the pretty teacher, and it would be fun to meet the girls again at the corner, and for them to tell each other what they had done during Christmas week. Alice, Bronwyn, and Edna lived on the other side of town, so it just happened that Aniela didn't see them very often except in school and during the little walk to and from the corner where they met and parted nearly every day.

It was still damp and misty when Aniela was ready to go to school, but the rain had stopped. She thought for a moment that Tatuś called her as she ran eagerly through the gate, but made herself believe that she had not heard the word "rubbers." She ran down the hilly street just as Sue and Cecilia came down from the other side. They met where the two streets joined and went together toward school.

By the time they reached the pavement on Main Street, Aniela's shoes were wet and full of mud. She wished she had gone back to put her rubbers on, but it was too late now.

School began with "The Star Spangled Banner." Aniela loved to sing. She didn't know what "ramparts we watch" meant, but when it came to the part about "the land of the free and the home of the brave," she knew what that meant, for Father had told her that it means America. She sang at the top of her lungs.

The spelling and arithmetic were just as hard as she thought they would be, but soon it was time for recess, time for tag and time for talk.

In the afternoon Miss Bauer, the teacher, began the geography lesson. They were studying the countries of middle Europe.

"I think it would be a very good idea," she began, "for us to find a new way to study our geography. We could work out a kind of plan about something special. We could call it a 'project.' Suppose each of you choose a country and find out all you can about it. There will be extra credit for unusual things that you find out for yourselves. You can get your parents to help you and you can go to the library, where I know Miss Patterson will help you find books that you need.

"Perhaps some of you can dress in the costume of the country you have chosen. Perhaps you can bring some special kind of food from that country and we could have a kind of party. Would you like that?"

There was so much clapping of hands to show how well they liked it that Miss Bauer had to wait until it was quiet to begin again.

"Now, each of you in turn can tell me which country you have chosen, and I will write it on the board. Then we won't have too many people choosing the same country. Michael, you begin. Then we will go right down the row to the back and up to the front again."

Michael chose Slovakia. Miss Bauer wrote his name on the board with Slovakia after it. When it came to Sue she chose Bohemia. Alice chose England and Bronwyn chose Wales. Cecilia's turn came before Aniela's. She chose Poland.

Aniela looked disappointed.

Then it was her turn to choose.

"I was going to choose Poland," she said.

"You may have Poland, too, if you like," said Miss Bauer. "You may find some things that Cecilia won't find." She wrote Poland after Aniela's name.

The girls walked from the school with their arms around each other. There was so much to talk about: all the Christmas holidays, and what fun they'd had; and all about the new project and the costumes they would wear at the party. While Aniela and Cecilia were talking of their Polish costumes for the project, they spoke so many words in Polish that Alice said:

"How can you understand such a language? It sounds to me like Ppsh-wsh-psh-wsh!" She made "shhushhing" sounds with her lips, then she stopped, put one hand on her hip, and pointing to the window they were passing, she said:

"And look at that name! Now who could ever say a name that begins with S-z-c-z all together with no letters in between?"

They all laughed, Cecilia and Aniela loudest of all.

"Oh, it's easy!" Aniela said. "You can say fresh cherries, can't you?" Alice nodded. "Well," Aniela went on, "it is just the same. Sh-ch! That's all there is to it. And *y* is like *i*, and when you see a tail under a letter, it means you put an *n* in. It is easy!"

"Easy for *you*, you mean!" Alice answered. Then they talked about how hard it is to learn English, never knowing where the accent should go, and Aniela told them how much trouble she had with "through," "tough," and "trough," and how hard it was for her to spell words with *e* and *i* together. They reached the corner and it was time to part.

Aniela could hardly wait to tell Papa and Mama about the project.

When she reached the corner, she ran the rest of the way, through the gate, up the steps, and was calling, even before the door banged shut:

"Papa! Papa! Are you here?"

She needn't have shouted. There sat Papa looking at her over his glasses. Aniela laughed and ran to him, but Papa held her off and looked down at her wet, muddy shoes.

"Well, my little one," he said, "what do you think Mamusia is going to say to that? Do you think it is for you to be so careless that she works so hard?"

"Oh, Tatuś," Aniela begged, putting her arms around his neck, "don't tell. Please, Tatuś, Tatusienko!! *Please!* I'll take them off and put them to dry by the fire, and Mamusia will never know." Aniela sneezed.

"Oh, yes, she will know all right enough. But why didn't you wear the rubber overshoes she bought for you?" he asked. "I reminded you, do you remember?"

"Yes, Tatuś, but I didn't think." Aniela hung her head again.

"You are a true Pole. You know that old saying, 'A Pole thinks after his head is cut off!' Your mother will have to attend to that cold you have. Off with those wet shoes and get yourself dry stockings, too." Papa left his work and found some of Babcia's goose grease which he rubbed into the leather of Aniela's shoes to keep them from getting stiff and squeaky. Aniela went upstairs to get an old pair of stockings. She thought she would wait until Mama came home to tell about the project.

Chapter Four

THE NEXT FEW DAYS Aniela tried not to let Mama know that she had a cold, but she couldn't keep from sneezing and coughing. One night Mama rubbed her throat with goose grease and told her to wrap her stocking around it. But still she coughed. Mama came up the stairs with the lamp and rubbed Aniela's chest again with the grease.

"Is this to keep *me* from squeaking?" Aniela tried to make Mama laugh, but Mama was not in a laughing humor.

"There!" she said, pulling up the quilt. "Perhaps that will stop your coughing. Making yourself sick doesn't help your Mamusia very much. You squeak already." She tucked the quilt around Aniela's back, and, taking the lamp, went downstairs.

Aniela kept very quiet. She couldn't go to sleep when she thought how unhappy she would be if she were *really* sick and couldn't go to school. Then she wouldn't be able to practice the folk dances. She couldn't go to the library with the girls. They might even have the project without her!

She looked at the shadow where the Queen of Heaven stood in her little house and said her prayers again. Perhaps she would be all right in the morning.

When Mama came to wake her in the morning, she loosened the stocking around Aniela's neck, and, holding the lamp close, looked at her throat.

"No school for you today, my Anielcia. Stay in the house and keep warm, then perhaps by tomorrow you can go. Now I am leaving for work. Take good care, and keep away from the cold, but get yourself dressed and downstairs."

At school time Aniela stood at the window. Sometimes it was fun to be out of school, but now she looked longingly out of the window as the boys and girls ran down the hill and wished she were with them. It was so exciting to talk about the "project."

Father came in from the back yard.

"Well, my Anielcia, you are wishing to go to school, aren't you? What did I tell you? After the trouble comes, then one begins to think, isn't that so?" He put his arm around Aniela's shoulders and drew her away from the cold window.

"Come, child," he said. "Find something to work at. Aren't you doing some kind of fancywork? Besides, there is plenty of other work to do." He looked at the clock and went on:

"Now it is time for me to go and attend to some work. While I am gone, you tidy the house. Then when I come back we could talk of the project thing you were telling Mamusia about."

Aniela thought about all the things Mama would like her to do. Suddenly it seemed interesting to see how well she could make a bed. And it was fun to show Papa how neat she could make the kitchen. She washed up the coffee cups that stood on the kitchen table, put away the bits of bread and coffee cake, then polished the stove. She straightened the cot on which Tadek slept, then went upstairs to tidy the bedrooms. She went first to Mama's room and pulled up the blind. It was creased and full of pinholes. She straightened the small lace curtain that hung from the sash and made the bed neatly. She went across the little platform at the top of the steps to her own room. It was very cold up there, and the window was covered with frost again. The oilcloth on the floor was worn where the boards were uneven and felt cold through the soles of Aniela's shoes. The bed linen was icy-cold as she smoothed and plumped the deep-piled pillows. The iron bed was cold when she touched it, but the Queen of Heaven smiled as warmly as ever from the rich, dark frame of polished wood. She straightened the little tin trunk under the window, then opened it to look again at the dress Mamusia said she could wear for the project. It was one Mama used to wear in the old country. It was gaily striped in orange, green, brown, and blue. There was red in it, too, and stripes of white. The bodice was embroidered, but Aniela couldn't help wishing it were spangled like the one Cecilia said she would wear.

She put the things back where she had found them and closed the lid of the little tin trunk just as she heard Papa come in. It took but a moment to finish hanging up her clothes, gather up her fancywork, and skip down where it was warmer.

Together Aniela and her father sat beside the cheerful, glowing heat: Papa with the music he was arranging, Aniela with her sewing; Papa smoking his pipe, and Aniela telling him about the party they would have at school when the project was complete.

"You know Cecilia says her dress is prettier than mine," said Aniela with a little pout. "She says there are spangles on the waist, and it is cut in a fancy pattern, and there are ribbons on the skirt. She says she has a wreath for her hair, too. I wish Mamusia's dress had spangles on it. I wish I had flowers for my hair." Aniela looked at her father as if she was sure he could make it all as she wanted it. Papa looked up, puffed on his pipe a moment, then said:

"Oh, you mean Cecilia Święcicka? Her papa and mama come from Kraków. That dress is from Kraków. That is why it is so." He went on smoking and making little black notes on the music paper. Then he laid down his pipe, and began again.

"You know Mamusia comes from Łowicz, the very heart of Poland. There,

39

LIBRARY

COLLEGE OF ST. BENEDICT

St. Joseph, Minnesota 56374

90100

the little farms run out from the village in long, narrow stripes. There are fields of grain and green pastures with deep green hedgerows between. There are red-brown plowed fields and black bottom land; blue field flowers, red poppies, and white daisies. That is what your Mamusia's skirt means. The colors are from Mother Earth herself.''

Aniela opened her eyes in wonder.

"Why, I didn't know about that at all!"

"It is true, my little one."

"That will be something to tell Teacher about when we have the project," said Aniela, delighted. "No one else will have that to tell, I am sure. Maybe I can get a good mark for it. Now, I must write it all down so I won't forget it." She dropped her sewing and ran to get her copybook and pencil.

"Now, Tatuś, tell me again, so I get it all right." So Papa told her again. He reminded her, too, of the famous men and women Poland had given to the world: scientists, musicians, statesmen.

"You know Stan heard Paderewski play in Philadelphia not long ago. He wrote an article for the Polish paper about it, remember? He also wrote an article about Madame Curie and her husband and their discoveries in science. Chopin, who wrote such beautiful music, comes from the very province your mama comes from. Then, you mustn't forget to tell about Kościuszko, who helped to free the peasants. You know he and Pułaski helped George Washington during the American Revolution, too."

Aniela knew all about Kościuszko, of course. There he was on top of the bookcase — under him was Babcia's egg money.

"It is best that you go to the library and look up these names, then you will learn for yourself about them," said Papa.

Aniela so much enjoyed this visit with her father that the time flew and she didn't realize that it was noontime until he asked:

"Is there any coffee left? Didn't Mamusia leave some on the back of the stove? You know, there is a good story about coffee and how we come to have crescent rolls. I will tell you, but first let us see about something for us to eat. The cold weather makes me hungry."

While they ate, Papa told Aniela the story about the coffee and the crescent rolls.

"You know about the good King John, Aniela, and how he saved Christianity for Europe?" he began.

"Oh, yes, you mean Jan Sobieski. We learned that at the Saturday school," said Aniela,

"You see, the Turks would have taken all of Europe if he had not been so wonderful a general," Papa went on. "Poland was then a strong country, and the Turks could not get beyond her borders. But during this time, she had fought many wars to keep her freedom. She had fought Sweden and Russia as well as the Turks." Papa stopped to light his pipe, and Aniela asked:

"Is this a story about *coffee*, Papa?"

"Yes, oh, yes, just wait and you shall see," he went on. "The Turks had reached into Austria and were threatening the city of Vienna when the Emperor sought help from Poland. King John was no longer young, and he was weary of wars, but the Austrians begged his help, so he consented to go to their aid. When the Turks heard that Sobieski was on his way, they fled in terror, leaving behind them great quantities of coffee. Coffee had not been used in that part of Europe before that time.

"A Polish spy had carried information that led to the defeat of the Turks. He had learned their language and their way of living, so he knew the use of coffee. As a reward for his great service to the country, the Emperor gave him permission to open the first coffee shop in Vienna. To celebrate the victory, he made rolls to serve with the coffee in the shape of the crescent that to this day is the symbol of Turkey."

"And is *that* why we have crescent rolls?" Aniela asked in wonder.

"That is why," said Papa, slowly sipping his coffee.

"Will you soon be finished, Tatuś? Let's go back and talk some more about Poland, and let me write down the story about the coffee and the crescent rolls."

When Tadek came home, his face black with coal dust, except for his teeth and the whites of his eyes, Aniela had the top of the kitchen stove full of kettles,

heating water for him to bathe. She had put on the supper to heat, too, and when Mama opened the door, the house was filled with the smell of good food and with warmth. To be sure, Tadek's work clothes were just where he had taken them off and the tub of black water was standing in the kitchen, but Papa had put away his music and Aniela had set the table for supper. Mama was pleased.

Aniela went back to school the next day, but when she talked to the girls about the project she didn't tell them anything about her costume and its meaning, nor any of the things Father had told her. Those she would keep a secret until the day of the party. Mama said she would make crescent rolls and *pączki* doughnuts. Aniela longed for the day to come. But there was so much to do that the time passed quickly.

In the evenings, Tadek helped Aniela draw a colored map of Poland. When she had drawn it carefully, he showed her how to make the striped fields. Then he made pictures of the little thatched houses with flowers growing in front of

44

them, geese near the ponds, and peasants working in the fields.

"Now," said Aniela, "if you could only put a stork near the chimney!"

"Well," said Tadek, a little proud of what he had done, "I guess I can. I could make it look better if I had paints, but I guess I know what a stork looks like." He sharpened his pencil and drew as carefully as he could what he thought was a stork.

"To be sure," said Mama, "it looks a little like Babcia's gander." But Aniela thought it fine.

Papa wrote out for her another copy of the Christmas carol she loved so well. Tadek loved it, too, and decorated it with the birds singing. Aniela began to have quite a collection for her "project." She could hardly wait!

One evening after supper Sue came and asked Father to help her find some music. Everyone knew that Father had a great deal of music. Aniela wondered what she wanted it for, but Papa didn't say anything about it, and of course she couldn't ask.

Another time Michael came, and he and Papa sat over the table whispering and humming and writing for quite a while, but Aniela was told to keep herself busy in the kitchen, so she didn't know what it was all about. Of course many of the neighborhood people came to Papa for help about many things. He wrote and understood English better than some.

Finally the day came for the project and the party. Through the town from every direction came boys and girls in their chosen costumes. Most of them wore the dress that their parents had brought from the old country, and they carried in baskets the special food each was to bring.

Chapter Five

THE SINGING WAS LUSTIER than ever that morning. The "rocket's red glare" pierced the roof! It was hard to make arithmetic seem important, and spelling was even duller than before, but at last they were over.

Miss Bauer held up her hand for quiet.

"Now, boys and girls," she said, "you have all done so well in taking an interest in our plan that I think we shall begin to work it out right now. You have brought so much food that I am sure there is enough for another whole class so let us invite Miss Sadowska and her boys and girls, shall we?" Miss Bauer sent Aniela with the invitation. It took a little while to get all the children seated. Some sat two in a seat, some sat on the floor around the room.

"If we try," Miss Bauer began again, "I am sure we can be quiet enough to have our party and our lesson all at once." She opened a covered basket and showed them half-moon pies she had brought and told how the recipe had been handed down from mother to daughter for generations.

"And I have brought enough for everyone!" she said, smiling. "But pie is better for the last, so let us begin with some other food.

"Now, Michael, you are first on the list. Will you begin? Didn't I see a basket on your arm? You chose Slovakia, didn't you?"

"Yes, Miss Bauer," said Michael, answering all the questions at once. "My mother sent some sheep's milk cheese that she knows how to make."

"That will be very good," said Miss Bauer. "Did anyone bring bread?"

Cecilia had rye bread, and Aniela had her crescent rolls.

"Perhaps the rye bread will be best for this cheese, and since it is soft we can spread it with the knife I brought." Cecilia passed her basket of bread, and Aniela followed her with the jar of cheese while Michael began his story.

Michael looked very handsome in his sheepskin coat embroidered in bright colors, and with his broad red belt. Into the belt was thrust a hatchet. He began to speak.

"This is the way my father used to dress when he lived in the old country in the Carpathian Mountains in Slovakia. This hatchet was used for clearing the way and for help in climbing. It was always kept bright and sharp ready for use, my father says."

He held up the hatchet. Then he reached into his basket and brought out several things that looked strange and interesting and went on:

"My father says that the men and boys of his part of the country were skilled in wire work and made curious things of it. He says they used to go about among the peasants selling these things and mending broken dishes. Like this, see!" He held up a plate, around which was woven a close pattern of fine wire. It was so carefuly done that it looked as if the plate had been made that way in the beginning.

"This plate was broken into a dozen pieces," he said. "Yet you cannot see a crack." He looked very proud. All the boys and girls were so interested that they even stopped eating.

Then Michael held up a queer-looking contraption that was also made of woven wire.

"This is one of the things the wire boys sell. It is a mousetrap. No mouse can run free to eat up the food when one of these is in the house!" Everybody laughed. Then Michael said:

48

"My father taught me a song about the wire boys, and Aniela's father helped me to put it into English. Shall I sing it?" Michael was one of the choir boys, so he didn't mind singing.

"Why, that would be splendid!" said Miss Bauer. "Stand up and sing out so we can all hear the words." And here they are:

"This is the wire man,
He wires the dishes.
Who gives him a penny
Will gain his good wishes.

"This little wire boy
Everyone hears his hail,
Because he cries all the day,
'Mousetraps for sale!'

"This little wire boy
Comes from the mountain height.
All the day he wanders,
But he sleeps at night."

Everybody put down the bread and cheese to clap their hands. Aniela remembered hearing Babcia tell about the wire boys and how they mended her pots and dishes.

Then it was Sue's turn. Her costume was bright with embroidery, too. A kerchief covered her head as it did Aniela's. In her basket she had brought honey and sausage and bread.

She began to speak.

"My dress is from Bohemia," she said, then told where Bohemia lay in Europe and the countries that bounded it. She told how well kept the farms were and how fine the cities. She took out of her basket a beautiful little pitcher of ruby glass that her mother had brought from Bohemia where it was made.

"My father told me that some of the most beautiful glass in the world comes

49

from Bohemia." Sue held the little pitcher up for all to see.

Then she said: "Aniela's papa lent me a copy of our Bohemian song. Shall I sing it?"

"Oh, yes, please do," said Miss Bauer.

In her native tongue Sue sang "Where Is My Home?" Then Aniela knew what it was Sue had come to see Papa about. She could understand most of the words, because they were much like Polish words.

It was Alice's turn next. Alice had currant tea buns in her basket. She was dressed in her Sunday best and had her prettiest hair ribbon on. She had chosen England for her country. She told of what fine silver plate comes from England; what good, hand-woven cloth is made from the wool they raise there. She told of the beautiful dishes that are made in England, and how the old patterns for the dishes were brought from China three hundred years ago, and that is why it is called "chinaware." She told the story Miss Patterson had helped her find about the willow pattern that has been used a great deal and that we all know.

Bronwyn had chosen Wales. She had brought little meat pies, which Miss Bauer divided so there would be enough to go around. Bronwyn wore a thick, stiff dress of close-woven wool.

"It is good for keeping out the damp and cold," she said. "It is always damp and foggy some part of the day in Wales where we used to live."

She wore a kerchief crossed over her breast and a checked apron. On her head was a frilled white cap, on top of which was a steeple-crowned hat.

"And when the weather was very bad," she said, "we did this." She put on a great cape with an enormous hood that could be pulled up over steeple-crowned hat and all. Aniela thought she looked like the pictures of Mother Goose that she had seen in the first grade room.

Bronwyn told how her father had been a miner in Wales, as he was in

America; how proud he was of his own mining tools, and how the miners all depended on him. She told about the fine stone houses they had lived in. How they were built close together and went up and up the steep streets.

"A little like Pennsylvania houses," she said. "Only — different." Everybody laughed, even Bronwyn herself.

She told how they had come to America because wages had gone so low in their country and her father hoped for a better living here. When she described how the daffodils grew on the hillside in the spring, her chin trembled, because it made her homesick. She sat down. Then she remembered her cockle basket and got up again to tell how she used to visit her grandmother near the sea and

gather cockles on the shore. She said that cockles were small shellfish very good to eat.

"I am sure we should all love to go to Wales," said Miss Bauer. "That was a very good story, Bronwyn.

"Now, Cecilia, it is your turn. Didn't I see something else in your basket?" Cecilia brought out the pink slices of ham that were supposed to have been eaten with the bread, but Miss Bauer told Aniela to pass her crescent rolls instead. What a feast it was!

Cecilia looked just as pretty as Aniela thought she would. She wore the Krakowiak costume. The top part was a little jacket cut in tabs about the waist, with spangles sewed to the edge and around the square neck. Underneath the jacket was a white blouse with full sleeves like Aniela's. But the skirt, instead of being of striped wool, was of fine white material, with ribbons of every color running around the deep hem. She wore high red boots and on her head a wreath of flowers, with more ribbons streaming.

She told a great deal about the city of Kraków and about the dragon that Krakus killed. How he used to eat more and more people and animals until he was fed a sheepskin stuffed with sulphur, then he drank and drank of the river Vistula until he burst.

Then Cecilia read how Poland had always been a place of safety for those who were in trouble, how, during the time called the Reformation, books were allowed to be printed when they were forbidden in other countries of Europe. She told of the University of Kraków and that it was one of the oldest in Central Europe, about the wonderful cathedral of Kraków, the palaces and the gardens.

Aniela began to think it hardly worth while to tell what she knew but she and Cecilia and Michael danced the Krakowiak, as they had learned it at the Saturday school, and Miss Sadowska looked pleased.

Then, while the boys and girls were clapping, Aniela went back to her seat to get her things ready, for her name was next on the board.

She got out her copybook, in which was the Christmas carol, the story about her costume, and the one about the coffee and crescent rolls. She spread out the map and waited to be called upon. Before the room was quiet again, someone knocked at the door.

Miss Bauer held up her hand for silence and went to see who it was. It was a strange man. To Aniela, he looked like the man who had visited Father Witkowski at Christmas time and who came to the Saturday school entertainment. He talked in a low tone to Miss Bauer for a moment, then sat down near Miss Sadowska, whom he seemed to know.

"We have company, boys and girls, and I know you will want to share our party with him. Then, shall we go right on? Aniela, I think you are next," Miss Bauer said, as she arranged some of the food on a paper napkin for the stranger. Aniela wished she didn't have to tell her story with the strange man there, but he looked so friendly, and seemed to be having such a good time, that she began by opening her basket to bring out the *pączki*. Mama had made more than enough. The bottom of the basket was filled with the luscious-looking doughnuts. Miss Bauer took the basket to pass it around.

"My mamusia came from the province of Lowicz, in the heart of Poland. That is why my dress is like this instead of like Cecilia's! See! This is where it is," she held up the map and pointed out where Łowicz lay. Then she read the paper Father had helped her prepare, telling the meaning of her peasant's costume. She pointed out the yellow for the wheat field, the brown for the plowed furrows, the black for the bottom land. The green was for the grass where the cattle stood all day in the sun. The dark green was for the hedgerows of small trees and shrubs where the rabbits hide and birds have their nests.

Then she read what Miss Patterson had helped her find out about Chopin, the composer, and Paderewski, the great pianist, and how Stanisław had heard him play! Of course she remembered to tell about *Kościuszko*. She read what Father had told her about the victory of the Poles in a battle against the Turks.

"And that is why we have crescent rolls!" she said, as she finished her story. Then she asked Miss Bauer if they couldn't all sing the carol Tadek had decorated, even though Christmas was long past. Many of them knew it from having learned it at the Saturday school.

"There is always time for a song," said Miss Bauer.

Aniela began:

When they had finished singing the carol, Miss Bauer called them to attention again.

"Now, boys and girls, there are only a few more to tell their stories. Then it will be time to go home. Gather up all of your things that belong to the lesson, and Aniela, you can collect them for me to see. I know you have maps and pictures and your stories, and I shall look them all over carefully."

While the last two boys were telling their stories, one about Lithuania and the other about Russia, Miss Bauer and some of the girls passed around the half-moon pies.

The party was nearly over. Aniela sighed. It had been such fun!

Then Miss Bauer spoke to her.

"Aniela, will you stay for a few moments after the others have gone?"

Aniela looked surprised. What could Miss Bauer want her for? Didn't she like her part of the "project"?

Finally, Miss Bauer came back to where she sat and said: "Aniela, you have told us many things about Poland that I am sure we should never find in books. We shall think of Poland as our friend more than ever. Come up here to the front of the room. Here is someone who would like to speak to you." She took Aniela by the hand and led her over to Miss Sadowska and the strange visitor.

"Do you know that your dress is just like the one my mother used to wear in Poland?" the stranger asked Aniela. "*I* come from Łowicz, too! And how that dress and kerchief take me back! I am glad you know the meaning of it. When I am painting the picture on the church wall, I shall think of you in that little kerchief." He pinched Aniela's cheek.

Aniela's eyes opened wide. A painter! The very one who was painting the church wall? She could hardly believe it! Then he *was* the man that Father called "that painter fellow"! How she wished that Tadek could be there!

Quick as a wink she thought, "If he likes my dress, perhaps he will like me, too, and will listen if I tell him about how Tadek wants to paint." She began to say it all at once, as if she were afraid he could get away before she finished.

"My brother—he can draw. He can paint, too, if he has paints. He thinks all the time about drawing and painting. He works in the mine and drives Rosie, but nights, when supper is over, he draws pictures. He draws everything!"

She stopped for breath. She looked at Miss Bauer, afraid she had said too much, but Miss Bauer was smiling and handing to the painter the carol they had sung. The painter was smiling, too, and when he saw the carol, he looked at it for a long time. Then he said:

"So your brother did this?"

Aniela nodded. Her words were all gone.

"It is beautiful," said the painter. "But who is Rosie?" His eyes twinkled at Aniela.

"Rosie is the mine mule," she answered. "And sometimes she balks."

"Yes, I know about mine mules. I used to drive one myself. I was just teasing. Now tell me more about this brother of yours." He looked again at the

p Gaily
mf
Lo! on this first Christmas Day- All the world is Bright and gay-
Hark, the nightin-gale's sweet treble, while the goldfinch sings the al-to,
f
ff
And the birdies are a'winging, for the Babe glad carols singing
Old friend starling, he's the tenor, and the pigeon coos the basso
p
rall.
ca - rols sing - ing
coos the bas - so

carol of the birds. "When he can draw like this, he should find an easier way to make a living than working in a mine. He has a real gift. I should like to see this boy. And doesn't your father play the organ? Doesn't he want your brother to learn to draw and paint!"

Aniela hung her head. She didn't want to say anything against her dear, dearest papa, so she didn't say anything for a moment. Then:

"Mamusia wants Tadek to paint more than anything, but Tatuś says he can't make a good living that way," she said.

"But a gift like this must not be buried. Perhaps your daddy is right. There aren't always churches to be painted. Sometimes painters do go hungry. But if that is what you want most, to draw and paint is like having food and drink. Something must be done. I shall talk to this daddy of yours, then we shall see!" He smiled at Aniela.

Something bubbled up inside her. Something wonderful was going to happen! She knew it!

Aniela suddenly felt she must get home. She must tell someone or she would burst! She picked up her basket and her shawl, and without stopping to say "Goodbye," ran as fast as she could go out of the school and up the street, around the corner and up the hill toward home.

Chapter Six

AS SOON as she opened the door, Aniela knew that Mamusia was home. The house was always different in some way when her mother was there. Mama answered her call from the kitchen. Aniela was so out of breath at first that she couldn't say a word, but Mama knew from her radiant look that something pleasant had happened.

"Oh, Mamusia!" Aniela gasped. "It was wonderful! We had such a good time. Everybody was dressed up, and they told such interesting things! But — best of all — what do you *think?* You can't guess!" Aniela teased Mama for a moment, dancing around her, then gently pushing her toward a chair, where she sat down, looking at Aniela's happy face.

"This is what happened. The painter who is making the picture on the wall of the church came to the school to our party! He saw the pictures Tadek made to decorate the Christmas carol, and the map, and he is going to talk to Daddy about helping him! What do you think of that? And he said my costume was just like the one his mother used to wear, and he said he would remember me." Then Aniela danced again around the kitchen, while Mamusia sat with the spoon in one hand and the corner of her apron in the other, smiling and tearful.

Just then Tad came in the door. He no sooner saw Aniela in her colorful dress than he began to plan how he could make a picture of her, with Mamusia sitting close by. He scarcely heard Aniela talking as she tumbled out the words and tried to tell him about the party, about the "project," and, saving the best until last, about the painter. Tadek saw her glowing face, saw her flying skirts as she danced about him, saw the lamplight on Mamusia's face, but when Aniela said, "Isn't it wonderful?" he answered. "Hmmmm? *What* is wonderful?"

He hadn't heard a word! Aniela was out of patience, but Mama only laughed at him and said, "You are the true dreamer, my Tad. Always your head is in the clouds. Here Aniela tells you wonderful news, and you haven't even heard her!"

Tadek grinned. He was used to being teased, and it bothered him not at all.

"Come on," he said. "What's the news?" So Aniela told him all over again, but before she was through Father came in.

"Supper waits," Mama said. "So wash up and we shall talk while we sit at the table." While Tad was washing, Aniela went up to put on her everyday clothes, and when she came down, all was ready.

Tad was so excited he could hardly eat. Father had seen the painter, too, and brought a message from him.

"This painter fellow," Daddy began as usual, "wants you to come and see him. You are to bring all the drawings you have, and let him see just what you can do. But all this talk of making a living with painting — I don't know. It may be all right, but maybe not.

"If you stay in the mine, after a while you make a *good* living. But not always are there churches to be painted. Look at me! I come to America and think everybody wants to pay money to learn music, but it is not so. Yet that is all I know how to do. If you leave the mine and learn painting, maybe sometimes you have a good living and maybe sometimes no living at all. But——" Papa shrugged his shoulders — "if Mamusia wants it and Tadek thinks it will make him happy — let him try it. He can still work in the mine while he is beginning, anyway. That painter fellow says you can come to see him tomorrow."

Tad said little, thinking how hard he would work. "Perhaps," he said, "I can go to Philadelphia like Stan and study there. Perhaps, oh, perhaps — *any-thing*." He began to eat as fast as he could so he could get to work. He started to lay out paper and pencils as soon as the table was cleared, but kept getting up out of his chair to find another drawing he had just remembered. Aniela followed him wherever he went. "Sit down and be quiet!" Tad said finally. Just as if he hadn't been running all over the house himself!

Mama sat under the light trying to lengthen the sleeves of Tad's jacket. He had grown so fast that there was a great gap of bare wrist between his sleeves and his mittens.

Father was reading aloud from the Polish paper an article that Stan had written.

Suddenly there was a knock at the door.

"Come in! Come in!" called Mama, getting up as the door opened and Mrs. Bartoszek came in.

"May He be praised!" she said, bowing as she closed the door.

"Forever and ever," answered Mama and Papa at the same time. Tad and Aniela got up to offer their chairs, and Father, getting up, offered his.

"No, no, do not disturb yourselves," she said. "I am not going to stay. I have a letter from *my* boy! Will you read it for me?"

"You must sit down for a moment," said Mama, "or you will take the luck out of the house. Come, sit down here." She made Mrs. Bartoszek sit in her chair and went immediately to put on the coffeepot.

"One gets lonely sitting at home so much," said Mrs. Bartoszek. "My son has been gone so long! Almost two years." Poor Mrs. Bartoszek wiped her eyes.

Papa read the letter. Then Mama brought in the coffee. Mrs. Bartoszek dried her eyes and soon she was as cheerful as ever.

" Aniela, child," she asked, "have you more of Babcia's eggs for sale?"

63

"No, Mrs. Bartoszek, but I will go for them in the morning," said Aniela. "Babcia said there would be some ready for me." Aniela was pleased. Her little hoard of pennies was growing!

The next day was Saturday, so Aniela set off early for Babcia's, stopping on her way for Saturday school.

Tadek's work in the mine was over at noon. Mamusia helped him get ready to visit the painter. She put his sketches in a neat package, then watched him as he went down the street.

The painter was high up on the ladder when he went into the church. There were many people going in and out so when Tad tiptoed in the painter paid no attention to him, but went right on with his work. Tad waited and waited. He twisted and turned. He scuffled his feet, and finally said loudly:

"Ahem!"

At the sound he was so frightened that he started to go without seeing the painter at all, but as he looked up the painter looked down and realized that Tad was there waiting to see him. He came down off the ladder and held out his hand.

"You are the boy who wants to paint, aren't you? You look like that pretty sister of yours."

Tad nodded and tried to shake hands and open the package of sketches all at once. The papers slipped away from him and sailed all over the stone floor. They both laughed, and that made them friends at once. The painter helped to pick them up, stopping to look at each one. Tad couldn't tell whether he liked them or not.

"You have a feeling for line," said the painter, "and should make good etchings." He continued to look at the drawing.

Tad hadn't the least idea what he was talking about.

"I meant by that," the painter went on, "you are able to tell a great deal

about a thing in the way you draw a single line. It is a gift you have that many never learn. Etching is an art that will make the most of your gift. But first you must practice drawing. Do as you are doing now, only when you draw a person, try to get someone to sit for you so you will see how their bodies are constructed. Practice will do it, and I shall help you. Then we shall see."

Tadek felt as if suddenly his whole life had begun anew. Everything looked different. This was the same church he had always known, where Father played the organ *each day*, where the same pastor was attending to his duties as usual. Yet it was different. The people were still going in and out, at the back, walking up and down the aisle, not even seeing the painter and Tadek, not dreaming that everything looked new and strange! Then he remembered that he hadn't answered, hadn't thanked the painter for his trouble and time.

"Oh, I shall practice," he said. "I shall draw every night."

"That is the only way," answered the painter. "And if you will bring me what you do, I shall tell you how to go on with it and improve it." He went on working, sometimes with his right hand, sometimes with his left.

"You may stay a while if you like. We are far enough away from the rest of the church so our talking will not disturb anyone. I can go right on with my work and talk at the same time." He went on almost as if he were talking to himself. "It doesn't matter *what* you draw, so long as you show that you are interested in drawing it. It is the *way* you do it that counts. If you make a picture of the miners coming home from work, you must show how tired they look. You must *feel* how tired they are, and you must show it somehow in your work."

Tadek had never been so happy in all his life. He wanted to stay there and watch the painter working and hear him talk, yet his fingers fairly itched to be drawing.

The painter talked on and on. Tadek sat down in a pew without knowing

67

that he sat down. Sometimes the painter said things he didn't understand, sometimes he said things that Tadek had always known but didn't know how to say. Suddenly the afternoon was gone.

"Another day is finished," the painter said, "but we are getting there. This wall is supposed to be finished by Easter, and if all goes well, it will be. Now, my boy, keep working. Come to my house Friday evening and show me what you have done." He pulled the cover over the picture and smiled. "Till Friday then?"

"Till Friday!" Tadek answered.

Wings seemed to lift Tad's feet as he ran up the hill.

Aniela had news, too. The teacher of the Saturday school had arranged with Miss Bauer to have the "project" repeated for the benefit of the "Freedom Fund." Everybody was invited and could give whatever he liked. There would be dancing for the young people besides, and Father and the others of the quartet would furnish the music. They had promised. There was to be an exhibition of the handwork they had done. It would be a wonderful party.

Aniela wanted to hear Tad's story, but she also wanted to tell hers, so the two stories were told together like this:

"What was he like? Did he say you make good drawings?" Aniela asked first. "What are you going to do? Are you going to begin *now* to paint?" But she didn't give Tadek a chance to reply before she went on:

"There's going to be a wonderful party at the Saturday school! We're going to——" But here Tadek interrupted, holding up his hand to stop Aniela's torrent of words.

"He says I have a 'feeling for line!' Ahem!" Tad put his thumbs in his suspenders and strutted with his cap over one eye, to show Aniela how important he was, and how much he knew. "And he says I can do etchings!"

Tadek hadn't any idea as yet what an "etching" was, but he knew Aniela would think it a big word and be impressed by how smart he was. She looked puzzled for a moment, then burst out:

"We're going to give the 'project' for all the parents and anybody who will come, and we're going to do the dances, and we're going to sing a lot of the songs, and——" But Tadek couldn't stand keeping his news to himself, and when Aniela had to stop to take a breath, he broke in with:

"And the painter told me to have people sit for me, so you will have to do it, Aniela, and he said that I should paint everything I see that I find interesting,

and I shall paint the river and the mine shaft and Babcia and Dziadek and Tatuś and——"

Aniela exclaimed:

"How wonderful! And shall I wear Mamusia's dress? I am to wear it again at the party." Just then Mama came in from the yard. At least she would be quiet long enough for Tadek to tell everything! Mama's face was rosy from the February wind and was wreathed in smiles when she saw Tad so happy. Without a word she put her arms around him, but Tad was not fond of being hugged and struggled to be free. Mama sat herself down and said:

"Tell me all about it, Tad. Aniela has chattered long enough."

While Tad talked he was searching in the bottom of the bookcase for paper and pencils. He must begin. He must begin *now!* Mamusia looked so pleasant with her cheeks rosy and her eyes glowing. He must try to put it down, now, before he forgot how she had looked when she came into the house. His talk dwindled away, for already his mind was on the picture. Aniela began again.

"Will you make crescent rolls again for the party, Mama? Please, Mamusia!" Aniela's arms were around Mama's neck, and she laid her head on Mama's

shoulder. Mama just looked down at her with a teasing smile.

"Don't move!" said Tad, holding up his head. "Don't move! That is what I shall draw first. You, Mamusia, with Aniela. It is like a Madonna picture."

He began to draw swiftly to get lines of the two figures before they should move, and to remember it he shut his eyes for a second.

He was so intent on what he was doing that he didn't notice when Mama and Aniela got up to get the supper ready, and only looked up when Father came in.

"So now you are a painter, I suppose?" Papa teased him. But Tadek only shook his head and went on with his drawing. Papa tousled his head and let him alone.

The party for the "Freedom Fund" was held early the next week. It was a very happy evening for Aniela. There was her fancywork up on the wall with the others, and pinned to the corner was a blue ribbon! That meant it was especially well done.

Aniela told her story about Poland even better than before and danced the *Krakowiak* until she was breathless.

Aniela was sure there had never been so fine a party. She didn't mind that the next day was the beginning of Lent, when she must go without many of the things she liked. There would be no parties with good things to eat. At home there would be fish, *fish!* But at the end of Lent there would be Easter, the loveliest day of the year.

Bitter winter weather brought more snow and sleet; kept Father busier than ever at the woodpile; made the hills slippery for walking but good for sledding. It set Tad thinking of how he could put the storm down on paper. He tried to show how the wind blew, with bending trees, blowing skirts, and flying scarves.

When he saw the drawing, the painter said: "But you forget that when there is snow on the ground you can't see *all* of a person's shoes. Show how the snow clings in little patches and how it goes over the soles."

"Yes, I remember now." Tadek nodded. "It sticks to my boots then melts and runs off on Mama's floor!"

Once, during the cold weather, Father invited some of his friends to play

string quartets. Mr. Świderski played the violin, Mr. Kulpinski the viola, and Mr. Wijek second violin. Father, of course, played the cello. Tad watched as they settled themselves in the center of the room where the hanging lamp lighted their music.

Aniela sat in the kitchen with Mama. She loved to hear them discuss what they should play first, Haydn or Mozart, Brahms or Schubert. She was allowed to stay up a little later than usual because there was no school the next day. She helped Mama make piles of sandwiches of different kinds of cheese and sardines and smoked fish, and a great pot of coffee. It was fun to taste each kind and to put them in heaps upon the plates. Then she was sent off to bed and went to sleep, cradled in sound. Sometimes, when the music grew louder, she wakened for a moment, but only long enough to feel the comfort of harmony, then was deep in dreams again.

Tad sat for a while at the table making designs for the Easter eggs he wanted to sell, but he kept watching how Mr. Świderski's hands held the bow, how Father pouted his lips when he played, how Mr. Wijek's hair grew stiffly up from his forehead. He reached for another piece of paper and began to sketch the quartet.

Chapter Seven

FEBRUARY finally blew itself out and March came in, warm and sunny. Buds began to swell, the willows put on a yellow mist, and down in the meadow, where the creek flowed free again, spring flowers bloomed. Tadek took pencil and paper with him on a Sunday afternoon walk and sketched the tumbledown sheds that stood beside the creek. Aniela wanted to take off her long winter underwear, but Mama wouldn't let her, and a good thing it was, for cold, wintry days came again, and the warm stove felt good, especially after Mama kept the windows open while she cleaned the house.

Aniela carried water from the pump until her arms ached. She scrubbed with the brush until it was worn down almost to the wood, but still Mama found more to do. The windowpanes were so bright and clear it looked almost as if they weren't there, and the sash curtains were clean and so stiff with starch that they stood out like Aniela's petticoats. The woodwork was scrubbed until the paint was gone around the doorknobs and on the window sills. The stoves were blackened and polished and the bright trim rubbed until it glittered.

Mama's house plants stood on the floor away from the cold, but where the sun could reach them, so they would be blooming for Easter.

Every night Aniela and Mama quickly cleared the table, so that Tad could have it for his work. Father often sat at the other end to write the parts he had arranged for the Easter music. Sometimes he got out the cello and tried over the parts. When Father played, the music made Tad's pencil fly and Aniela's needle go in and out faster than ever on the new embroidery she was doing.

Sometimes Mama stopped to look at her work, and once she said:

"Be careful, child, you are going over the line there! Go slowly. Now, you had better take out that last bit."

Aniela heaved a great sigh. Take out all those tiny stitches?

"Oh Mama, must I?" she begged. "I will *never* get it done!"

"You know the old saying," Mama said firmly. " 'Whatever is done in a hurry, is done in the Evil One's fashion!' "

Aniela began to rip out the stitches. She looked at Tad, who never seemed to tire of his drawing but patiently worked and rubbed it out when it did not please him, then drew it again. It was not perfect, of course, but when he had finished, it was the best he could do.

Already he was doing better work. When he wanted to draw one of the miners he looked at Father as the painter had told him to do to see how a man should look. Sometimes he talked out what he was thinking to Aniela.

"See how much broader Tatuś is across the shoulders than Mamusia," he would say. See how much bigger his hands are, and how much stronger his features." Aniela didn't understand all he said, but it sounded as if he knew a great deal.

Once he had made a sketch of Babcia feeding her geese. He showed her round, plump face with the kerchief tied under her chin. He drew it in pencil but in his mind he painted it in color. The painter liked that one especially.

Mama was making a new dress for Aniela so she would be gay and bright for Easter.

"All the world puts on a new spring dress for that happy day," said Mama.

"And it is right that we should be bright and gay, too, if we are able." When Aniela tried the dress on, she didn't want to take it off.

On the way from school the next day she told the girls about how pretty it was. Cecilia said she would have a new dress for Easter too, and Sue said, "Oh, so have *I* got a new dress."

"I'm going to have a new hat," Cecilia said. "A big wide one with roses on it."

They stopped to look in the milliner's window and choose which hats they liked best. Straw hats seemed a little out of place when it was so cold, but when Aniela was telling Mama about the ones they had seen, she said, "Easter is early this year, and if it is this cold, straw hats will look silly, but I guess women's pride will keep them warm. I suppose since the other girls are having new hats, you want one, too, is that it?"

"Could I have one, *could* I, Mamusia? Could it be a straw-colored one with blue flowers to match my dress? Please, Mamusia!" Aniela put her arms coaxingly around Mamusia's broad waist. Mama gave her a spank and said, as she changed her cold iron for a hot one: "Go on with your dear mamusias. Am I only your 'dear mamusia' when you want something, then?"

Oh, no, Mamusia, oh, no, you are always my dear mamusia. But — *could* I have a new hat?"

"We shall see, my Anielcia; perhaps, but these spring hats cost so much. Right now iron these last curtains for me." She went on with her other work while Aniela ironed.

When Father came he brought a letter from Stan. It was easier for Papa to read, so he opened it, and something fell out of the envelope.

"Money," said Papa. "It is a money order! Since when has Stan had money to send home to you?"

"Read! Read!" said Mama. "Read and find out!"

Papa read the letter. In it Stan told how hard he was working to get through by June. How he had been appointed to stay at the University hospital as interne, and how he had earned some extra money, teaching.

"So," he wrote, "I am sending a little present for you, my sister, for Easter, since I cannot come home. Use the money any way you like."

Papa handed the money order to Mama, who looked at it in wonder.

It had seemed so long to look ahead when Stan began his course at the University! Mama could scarcely believe that it was nearly over, the years had passed so quickly.

"Now," said Papa, "you can soon stop going to the factory. Stan will be a real doctor and will not need your help."

Aniela was disappointed that Stan was not coming home. He always came home for Easter. "But," she thought, "since he has sent Mama money, maybe she will take some of it to buy me a hat!" She went on thinking of those she had seen in the milliner's window and of which one she liked best. Then she remembered how long Mama had worn her old one, and how hard she had worked to help Stan through. She remembered how Tad wanted money for paints and how little she had saved in the pig bank. There were only thirty-six pennies! Tad had told her that one tube of oil paint was worth more than that!

She was ashamed, but she did want the new hat for Easter.

Mama and Papa bent over the money order.

"It says 'ten dollars,' " said Papa. "That's a lot of money for Easter." When Mama folded the little piece of green paper and put it away in her sewing box without saying anything, Aniela was sure there would be no new hat for her.

The days grew longer and the sun warmer. Mama's flowers began to open. The house was sweet with their odor. Every week Aniela had more eggs to sell.

Sometimes Dziadek brought them. Sometimes Aniela went for them.

Father had given Tad a whole list of orders for the eggs he was decorating. He worked at them every evening. When they were finished it was Holy Week and he took a pound of butter to carve a lamb for Easter. He followed a picture Mama had of the lamb with the cross. Mama put it in the cold where it would keep till the day before Easter when it would be put on the table with the other food to be blessed: the eggs, the salt, the bread, the sausage and the ham studded with cloves.

Every moment he could spare, Tad spent with the painter. Whenever he had an afternoon free, he was at the church, and once he came home so full of excitement that he took Mamusia by the arms and waltzed her around until she was dizzy.

"What do you think!" he exclaimed. "I really helped to paint the picture on the church wall! And what else do you think? The painter gave me some of his own paints! And wait till you see! Just wait! There is another surprise! You are to come early on Holy Thursday afternoon, and the painter will take the covering off and let you see the picture because it is something special. You'll see!" He let go of Mama suddenly and she almost fell into the chair, she was so dizzy. But he wouldn't tell what the surprise was.

When Thursday arrived, Mama came home from the mill at noon. Tad was home from his work, and he and Aniela were ready and waiting. Father had gone.

The painter was waiting for them and had moved the great cloth covering from the wall. In the picture at one side were the miners in their blackened clothes, their faces tired and dirty, looking toward a shining light.

At the other side was a field of waving grain with flowers growing at the edge, and standing knee deep in blossoms were happy people, men, women, and children, in the dress of the different countries from which they had come. They, too, were looking toward the light. There were Bohemians, Slovaks, Poles, and

Russians. There were Welsh and English, Scotch and Germans; all the many nationalities that go to make America.

Tad turned toward Aniela. Just then Father tiptoed from the chancel to stand beside her.

Tad looked at Mama to see what she would say.

But Mamusia said nothing.

She only stood still and looked at the picture. For there, right in front,

standing among the daisies, was her *own Aniela* in the striped Polish dress!

When they reached home Father said:

"This painting — I guess you are right, Mamusia. The boy should not be wasting his time in the mine. Stan is almost through. We can go on now to help Tad. The painter says he can get him into a school in Philadelphia if we can give him his living. I had hoped you could stop going to the factory soon, but——"

Mama's eyes grew brighter and brighter. She put her hand on Father's arm.

"The factory is nothing! What are a few years more? I won't mind. You will see!"

Tad looked at Mama, as Mama had looked at the painting.

Not one of them could say a single word! Papa wiped his nose and went to chop wood. Tad ran to help him. Mama bustled about getting supper, and Aniela ran upstairs to get the pennies she had saved.

Maybe there are more than I think, she hoped, but when she counted there were just as many as when she had counted them before. There were sixty. She thought of the hat in the milliner's window. How she wanted it! Before she had time to think of it again, she ran downstairs and emptied the pennies onto the table. Mama was surprised. She didn't know that Aniela was saving her egg money.

"You will not be sorry, my little one," she said. "This that you give to help your brother will come back to you many times over. Always we are happy when we do something for another."

All through the solemn three days before Easter Aniela remembered with quiet joy what she had seen in the painting. Beside the picture of herself there were the flowers in the field that Tad had painted. It didn't matter that Stan couldn't come home, it didn't matter that she hadn't a new hat. Even her new dress didn't matter so much now.

When she went to bed, she stood for a moment before the Queen of Heaven. In place of the faded paper flowers she put before her the blossoming star of Bethlehem she had found near the fence corner, to say she was thankful for all the good things that had happened.

Everything in the house was clean and ready for the Easter morning that dawned warm and beautiful. Before Aniela was quite dressed she looked out of the open window and saw Mrs. Bartoszek coming up the walk. She heard her open the door and call:

"The Lord is risen!" then heard Mama call back:

"He is risen indeed! Isn't this a beautiful Easter morning?"

"Beautiful indeed," said Mrs. Bartoszek. "More beautiful than you know! My son has come home! I just wanted to tell you." Aniela heard Mrs. Bartoszek go out and shut the door. All at once every bell in the little town began to ring. They pealed from the church around the corner where Father was already playing the organ. They rang from the steeple away up the other hill. They swelled in music from the spires down in the town, and from the little stone church farther on. They chimed from the little white church on Main Street and from the red brick church across the valley. Even the bells seemed to know that it was Easter morn!

Aniela was so stirred by the din of bells she could hardly fasten her starched petticoat. The new cashmere dress was ready over a chair and beside her brushed and polished old shoes lay a pair of new black stockings. Aniela wished she didn't have to tuck so much underwear into them, so they would look smooth and neat, but Mamusia was firm about it. She *had* to wear it.

The cool, smooth feeling of the cashmere and the soft ruching around her neck made her feel better, and when she peered into the cracked mirror, she looked so nice, it didn't matter that she must wear her old cap and coat.

"Come, Aniela," called Mama, "Tadek has gone, and Tatus has been at the church for a long time!" Aniela skipped down the stairs where Mama was waiting. As she reached the bottom, Mama looked her over well. She lifted the edge of Aniela's dress and petticoat to see if she was properly dressed, and said before she let her come through the doorway:

"Are you as clean all the way through as you are on top?"

Aniela bobbed her head and said: "Yes, Mamusia, do I look all right?" Mama still held her there, so Aniela knew there was something she wasn't telling. Aniela looked up. There it was! There on the bust of Kościuszko, making him look very

funny, was Aniela's spring hat! It was straw color, just as she wanted it, and on top were blue cornflowers.

Mamusia had a new hat, too. Hers was black and was trimmed with pink roses.

"Hurry! Hurry! Let's put them on!" cried Aniela. "Is mine on straight?" Aniela's hair was almost the color of the straw, and her eyes just matched the cornflowers. Mamusia's cheeks were pink like the roses on her hat.

Just as the bells stopped ringing two Easter bonnets went bobbing together through the church door.